Amazing Nature

Dramatic Displays

Tim Knight

Heinemann Library
Chicago, Illinois

Printed and bound in the Hong Kong, China by South China Printing

07 06 05 04 03
10 9 8 7 6 5 4 3 2 1

Library of Congress Cataloging-in-Publication Data

Knight, Tim.
    Dramatic displays / Tim Knight.
       p. cm. -- (Amazing nature)
    Includes index.
    Summary: Explores how different animals of the land, sea, and air create fantastic displays of light and color as they seek mates, give warnings, or simple gather together.
    ISBN 1-4034-0721-5 (hardcover)   ISBN 1-4034-3255-4 (paperback)
    1. Color-variation (Biology) 2. Display behavior in animals.
    [1. Color variation (Biology) 2. Animals--Habits and behavior.]
    I. Title. II. Series: Knight. Tim. Amazing nature.
    QH401.K57 2003
    591.4--dc21
                              2002153006

Acknowledgments
The publisher would like to thank the following for permission to reproduce photographs:
p. 4 Carl Boes/Bruce Coleman Inc.; p. 5 Douglas Faulkner/Photo Researchers, Inc.; p. 6 Chet Tussey/Gregory Ochocki Productions/Photo Researchers, Inc.; p. 7 Art Wolfe/Photo Researchers, Inc.; p. 8 Joyce and Frank Burek/Animals Animals; pp. 9, 11 Andrew J. Martinez/Photo Researchers, Inc.; pp. 10, 18 Mary Beth Angelo/Photo Researchers, Inc.; p. 12 M. Timothy O'Keefe/Bruce Coleman Inc.; p. 13 James Beveridge/Visuals Unlimited; p. 14 Charles V. Angelo/Photo Researchers, Inc.; p. 15 Ron Seston/Bruce Coleman Inc.; p. 16 David Hall/Photo Researchers, Inc.; p. 17 Chesher/Photo Researchers, Inc.; pp. 19, 20 Zig Leszczynski/Animals Animals; p. 21 Nancy Seston/Photo Researchers, Inc.; p. 22 Carl Roessler/Bruce Coleman Inc.; p. 23 Hal Beral/Visuals Unlimited; p. 24 Marian Bacon/Animals Animals; p. 25 Gregory G. Dimiji/Photo Researchers, Inc.; p. 26 Michele Westermorland; p. 27 P. Harrison/OSF/Animals Animals; p. 28 A. Flowers and L. Newman/Photo Researchers, Inc.; p. 29 Gregory Ochocki/Photo Researchers, Inc.

Cover photo: Gregory Ochocki/Photo Researchers, Inc.

Every effort has been made to contact copyright holders of any material reproduced in this book. Any omissions will be rectified in subsequent printings if notice is given to the publisher.

Some words are shown in bold, **like this.** You can find out what they mean by looking in the glossary.

Contents

The message

Animals and plants need to **communicate,** or share information, with each other. They do not use language like humans do. They have found other ways to pass on information. They send messages or attract attention by putting on a special show, known as a display. There are many different kinds of messages. When a male bird displays his colorful feathers to a female, he is saying "choose me" or "don't leave me." But a display to another male can mean: "I am stronger, so back off now."

The bright red body and wings of the scarlet tiger moth flash a clear warning. They tell hungry birds to leave the moth alone.

Many plants need animals to help spread their **pollen** and seeds. So they have colorful flowers to attract insects to their **nectar** and pollen. Plants often protect their seeds with a tasty fruit. When the animals eat the fruit, the seeds are taken to a new place to grow.

Some animals use bright colors to tell others to stay away. The colors warn attackers not to eat them because they taste bad or are poisonous.

Displays can be used to give wrong information. These displays can fool the listener or viewer. The yellow clearwing moth looks like a dangerous wasp. It also buzzes like a wasp. But really the moth has no stinger and cannot hurt others.

Messages like "look at me" or "don't touch!" may seem simple. But creatures have their own special way of sending these messages. And their displays are often very exciting to see or hear.

Heliconia, a kind of wild banana plant, has spiky, brightly colored flowers. These attract hummingbirds and other nectar drinkers that carry pollen from one plant to the next.

Saying Hello

Animals need to find **mates** so they can **reproduce**. They may also need to scare away a **rival**. It is important that animals **communicate**. An animal that wants to get the attention of another has to find the best way of saying "hello."

Male anole lizards signal to their rivals with colored throat flags.

Animals that live close enough to be seen by each other often just wave hello with a part of their body. Some lizards flash messages at each other with flaps of colored skin that flick out from under their chins. These are known as "throat flags." One of the male fiddler crab's front claws is much bigger and brighter than the other. To ask a female to join him, he stays near the front of his nest and then waves this giant claw in the air. These are all forms of **visual display**.

Using sound

Visual displays do not work for animals that live far apart or only come out at night. These creatures often use **vocal display** instead. They use their voices to send each other messages.

The bittern is a shy wading bird. During the day, it stays quietly hidden among tall water plants. But at night, its booming call can be heard at least a mile away. The six o'clock cicada is the noisiest insect in the Borneo rain forest. At around six o'clock, just when it is getting dark, the calls of the six o'clock cicada drown out all other sounds. The sounds are made by a pair of body parts called tymbals. These small, stiff flaps are attached to each side of its **abdomen**. The cicada flutters the tymbals against its body hundreds of times a second to make the sounds.

A male fiddler crab shows off his huge claw to all the nearby females.

Display of Strength

One of the main reasons animals display is to show enemies how strong they are. Male wild turkeys grow loose flaps of skin on their necks called wattles. The oldest and strongest birds have the biggest wattles. Younger males who meet these older birds will back down without a fight. The younger males know they would lose the fight if they tried.

A male hamadryas baboon yawns to display his sharp teeth.

Primate Links

When male baboons meet, they use visual signals to show who is boss. Older male gorillas avoid meeting by making as much noise as they can.

Old male silverback gorillas try to scare their enemies with displays of roaring, chest beating, and plant smashing.

Displays of strength are not just for **rivals**. Animals also send messages to more dangerous enemies. If a cobra feels it is in danger, it tries to make itself look bigger and more powerful. It rears up and spreads out its hood. A fully grown king cobra is about 13 feet (4 meters) long. When it lifts the front third of its body off the ground, it is as tall as a man. The cobra now looks much scarier. This is called a **threat display**. An enemy will leave quickly when faced with such a display.

A pack of African hunting dogs will try to pick out the weakest antelope in a herd. The dogs will then chase it until it is worn out. Instead of running away as the dogs get close, the antelopes put on a display. They leap high into the air and bounce around to show how strong they are. This display of leaping and jumping is called pronking or stotting. It is the antelopes' way of telling the hungry hunters to pick on someone else.

A king cobra raises its head and spreads its hood to show off its size and power. This sends an early warning that it is ready to attack.

Warning Colors

Putting on a special show for every enemy an animal meets can waste a lot of time and energy. Dangerous or poisonous animals often have special colors or markings on their bodies. These colors and markings send warnings to other creatures. The beautiful lionfish protects itself with the poison-tipped spines of its **dorsal fin**. Its red-and-white stripes tell other sea creatures to stay away.

The lionfish is one of the most poisonous creatures in the sea.

Most arrow-poison frogs are no bigger than a person's thumbnail. But their poison is so deadly that hunters use it on the tips of their blowpipe darts.

Watch out!

Most **amphibians** want to keep out of sight of any possible enemies. But tiny arrow-poison frogs sit calmly in the open. They shine like bright green, blue, orange, or yellow jewels. Their skins are coated in a deadly poison. For this reason, frog eaters have learned to leave them alone. Another poisonous amphibian, the fire salamander, has a yellow-and-black pattern that also warns hungry **predators.**

Cinnabar moth caterpillars eat a poisonous plant called ragwort. The poison does not hurt the moths. It just builds up in their bodies. This makes the caterpillars poisonous to anything that eats them. Their orange-and-black coloring is a warning. When they turn into moths, cinnabars are bright red and fly in broad daylight. Birds do not touch them. They have learned that colorful moths usually taste bad.

Bluffing

Brightly colored animals are not always scary or dangerous. Some of them just pretend to be. They are **bluffing**.

The milk snake is harmless. But it protects itself by looking almost exactly like the deadly, and very colorful, coral snake. Scientists call this **mimicry**. Hover flies and other insects that do not sting have the same yellow-and-black colors as dangerous wasps or hornets.

South American owl butterflies avoid bright sunlight. They fly mainly at dusk.

Owl Links

The owl butterfly and owl moth have something amazing in common. Both have **eyespots** on their wings that look like an owl's eye.

During the day, the owl moth rests with its wings spread out. If disturbed, it rocks back and forth instead of flying off.

The vampire squid changes the shape of its body to fool enemies. This strange creature turns itself inside out to show off a set of fake spines. These spines look hard and sharp, but they are as soft as jelly. Caterpillars twist their bodies into weird shapes. They can look like a tiny snake or arch their back like an angry cat.

Camouflage

Sometimes, the best choice is to pretend not to be there. Using **camouflage** is one of the best ways animals can make themselves seem invisible. They blend in with their surroundings by making themselves look like other objects. Rain forests are filled with hidden frogs, moths, crickets, and stick insects that look like leaves, twigs, moss, and thorns. Camouflage is their way of saying, "I'm not here."

The wings of this rain forest moth blend in perfectly with the dead leaves on which it has landed.

Surprise

Many animals protect themselves by surprising their attacker with a sudden display. Sometimes this scares away the enemy. Other times it gives the animal time to escape while the attacker is still surprised.

When something bothers it, a sun bittern fans out its tail and wings to show a pattern that looks like two giant eyes. It then walks toward the surprised attacker. Eyed hawk moths also flash a pair of false **eyespots** on their wings.

*The frilled lizard is a harmless Australian **reptile**. It scares attackers by puffing up the loose collar of skin around its neck.*

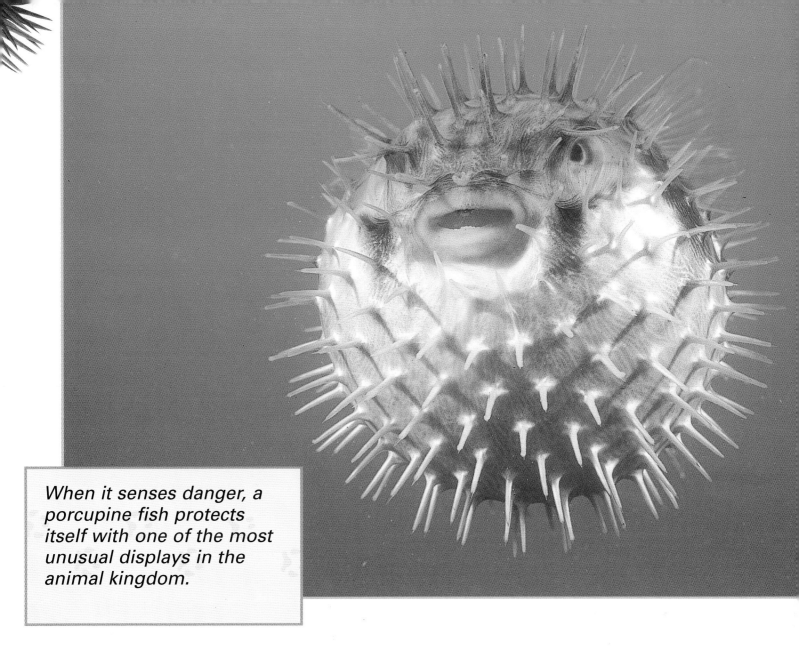

When it senses danger, a porcupine fish protects itself with one of the most unusual displays in the animal kingdom.

The blue-ringed octopus lives in shallow rock pools in Australia. It is very poisonous. When it is in danger, the rings on its arms turn bright blue. The fire-bellied toad flips onto its back and flashes its bright orange underside when attacked. The sudden color flashes shown by the octopus and toad remind enemies that these creatures are poisonous.

Sudden changes of shape can also be scary. The very poisonous porcupine fish blows itself up into a spiky balloon. By sucking in water, it can suddenly become much larger and look much more dangerous.

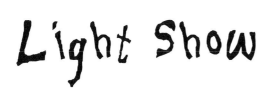

Light Show

Some animals only come out at night. Others live deep in the ocean where it is always dark. These animals display to each other with flashing lights. This is known as **bioluminescence.** This helps the animals hunt, keep away from trouble, or find a **mate.**

Fireflies have special light-making body parts on their undersides.

Many deep-sea creatures glow whenever they are bothered. They use bioluminescence to surprise their attacker and to give themselves time to escape. Firefleas are **microscopic** life-forms. They turn into glowing green sparks of light when a **predator** gets near. Some deep-sea squids make their getaway by dazzling an attacker with a cloud of light.

Fireflies are beetles that fly at night. They use their bodies as flashlights and flash messages to each other in the darkness.

Bioluminescence is used for hunting, too. One deep-sea angler fish attracts curious fish with its own flashing light. This light dangles like a glowing worm in front of its open jaws.

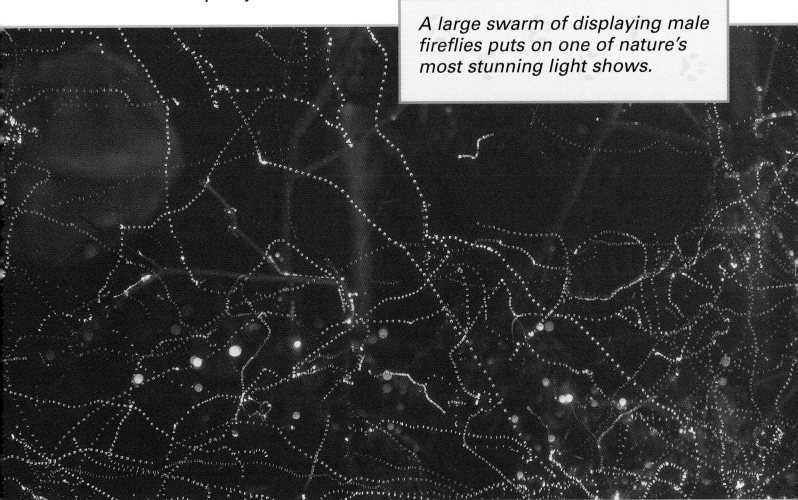

A large swarm of displaying male fireflies puts on one of nature's most stunning light shows.

Flower Power

Many flowering plants **reproduce** by using animals to carry their **pollen** to another plant of the same kind. In return, these animals get some of the pollen or a drink of sugary **nectar**. The plants use their flower displays to get the attention of birds and insects. Flowers have markings on their petals that point the way to the pollen. Some of these markings can be seen only by insects. They point toward the pollen or nectar, like arrows or landing lights on an airport runway.

Bright red displays tend to attract birds. Insects cannot see red colors clearly. The red-colored flower spikes of heliconias attract hummingbirds.

The bright red bottlebrush is a favorite of Australia's rainbow lorikeet birds.

Sunbirds drink from the blood-red flowers of the sausage tree but the first animals to visit are nectar-feeding bats. The flowers open at night and give off a bad smell that attracts bats and night insects. Flowers that display at night have a better chance of standing out from the crowd. They are usually white and stinky, so that thirsty visitors can find them in the dark.

Bee orchids use **mimicry** to attract insects. Their flowers look and smell like female bees. The male bee is fooled into thinking that he has found a female. He tries to **mate** with the orchid flower and pollen sticks to his body. When he flies off to a different flower, he moves the pollen to a new plant.

The titan arum, found only in Sumatra, Indonesia, has a spike of flowers 9 feet (3 meters) tall. Its outer cover looks like a giant trumpet.

Showing off

The animal kingdom is full of show-offs. Females are not just interested in good looks. They want a strong and healthy **mate**. Males often try to win a female by defeating their **rivals** or putting on a show.

Male helicopter damselflies fight over the pools of rainwater where a female will lay her eggs. After driving away his rivals, the winner floats over his tiny pond. He whirls his blue-tipped wings to get others to look at him. Male weaverbirds try even harder to get a female's attention. They build a nest. Then they show off their building skills by hanging underneath and flapping wildly. Kingfishers try to win over females by offering them food.

*Male humpback whales lift two thirds of their 55-ton (50-metric ton) bodies out of the ocean. Then they crash back in with a mighty splash. This **breaching** is part of their mating display.*

Flying tricks

Some birds do flying tricks. The male lilac-breasted roller tumbles and dives like a fighter pilot. He even does a victory roll. Ravens, fish eagles, and peregrine falcons also show off their flying skills to prove what good hunters they are. Sometimes the female joins in and the two birds dive-bomb each other. They often link feet or brush close together at high speed.

The widowbird has a strange courtship dance. He leaps into view above the long grass to attract females. Like other animal show-offs, he sends the message: "Look at me!"

A lilac-breasted roller launches itself into the air at the start of its display flight.

Beauty Contest

Many displays are meant to catch the eye of a **mate,** rather than show strength or skill. This is especially true in the bird world.

The male argus pheasant has extra-long wing feathers covered in spots. He clears a display area on the forest floor. He then dances for the females by spreading his wings and tail over his head like a jewel-covered fan.

A male frigatebird attracts his mate by puffing up a bright red pouch under his throat. He blows this up like a balloon, until the skin is stretched tight as a drum. Then he calls loudly as he bangs his outstretched wings against his throat pouch.

After puffing up his throat pouch, a male magnificent frigatebird tries to catch the eye of a passing female.

Some male birds of paradise display in groups. They flap their wings, fluff out their plumes, and scream loudly.

Birds of paradise live in New Guinea, an island in Southeast Asia with plenty of food and very few **predators.** The males spend most of their time trying to get the attention of females. Many of them have developed extra-long **plumes,** shimmering feathers, or weird head feathers. The males show off their stunning coat of feathers with an amazing variety of displays.

Courtship

Many animals keep displaying long after they have found a **mate**. This helps to strengthen the bond between the partners. They will stay together throughout the **breeding season**. In some cases they stay together for life.

Seabirds that nest in large **colonies** spend lots of time displaying to each other. The courtship display of the wandering albatross is the longest lasting bird dance in the world. When birds are old enough to mate, they join a colony and choose a partner. They display to each other for weeks. They rub and clap beaks together and point them to the sky while crying out loudly. From time to time, they stretch out their 9-foot (3-meter) wings and dance around each other. Two or three seasons may pass before they actually mate.

An albatross displays to its mate. It throws back its head and calls with its wings stretched out.

Every year, red-crowned cranes return to the same place to dance. They display to each other by bowing, leaping, and running.

Red-crowned cranes are famous for their graceful dancing display. At the beginning of spring, hundreds of birds flock to their frozen dancing grounds. Partners do a kind of "snow ballet." A pair of red-crowned cranes stays together for life. Their yearly dance helps them to keep their relationship strong.

The Greatest shows on Earth

Most displays have a special purpose, such as scaring enemies or attracting **mates**. But some of the most enjoyable things for people to see are huge groups of the same kind of animal traveling, resting, or feeding together. Many animals stay in groups because there is safety in numbers.

As darkness falls, 10 million bats leave one cave in Texas. There are so many that they turn the whole sky black. Also at dusk, flocks of scarlet ibis stop for the night in a swamp in Venezuela. The trees look like they are on fire because of the birds' eye-catching red feathers.

Scarlet ibis light up the sky as they return to roost for the night.

Australia's Great Barrier Reef is made up of coral animals. Once a year the corals put on a terrific fireworks display. The corals all **spawn** at the same time. Together, they shoot billions of eggs and **sperm** into the water. During this time, the sea looks like it is full of shooting stars and a billion tiny points of light.

Whenever animals gather in such large numbers, to sleep, rest, **hibernate,** feed, or **mate,** the sight can be truly wonderful.

The yearly spawning of corals on the Great Barrier Reef is an unforgettable sight.

Fact File

The booming call of the male kakapo, or owl parrot, from New Zealand can be heard up to 4 miles (6.5 kilometers) away by a female.

It takes a male frigatebird 20 minutes to puff up his display pouch.

Calfbirds got their name because the males display to a female by mooing like a cow.

When scared, the puffer fish can puff its body up to two to three times its normal size.

When in trouble, the horned frog of Central America puffs itself up and cries like a baby.

The orange, yellow, and black heliconius mimic is so similar to true heliconius butterflies that only an expert can tell them apart.

The tiniest drop of poison from the skin of an arrow-poison frog is enough to kill a human.

A New Guinea bird called the Vogelkop gardener builds a cave out of twigs. The cave is big enough for an adult human to crawl inside. The male decorates it with colorful objects to attract a female.

Glowworms feed on the insects that are attracted to the light they give off.

In the **breeding season** male and female great crested grebes (a type of diving bird) give each other weeds.

Blue-footed boobies "say hello" to each other by waving one of their feet.

When a male lyrebird displays, he does an excellent job of copying the calls of other birds as well as the noises of machines such as cameras and chainsaws.

When they are ready to **mate,** thousands of flamingos begin marching as a group across Africa's salt lakes.

Glossary

abdomen   third, or lower section, of an insect's body

amphibian   animal that can live in water and on land

bioluminescence   the giving off of light by a living thing

bluffing   pretending to be dangerous to fool enemies

breaching   leaping above the surface of the ocean

breeding season   time of year when animals **mate**

camouflage   disguise that helps an animal hide

colony   place where large numbers of the same animal gather to raise young

communicate   share information

dorsal fin   fin on the top of a fish

eyespot   marking that looks like an eye

hibernate   sleep through the winter

mate   partner. Also, what a male and female animal do to start an egg or baby growing inside the female.

microscopic   only visible through a microscope

mimicry   pretending to be a different animal or object

nectar   sugary liquid made by flowers

plume   large, eye-catching feather or tuft of feathers used for display

pollen   sticky powder made by flowers

predator   animal that hunts and kills other living creatures for food

reproduce   produce young

reptile   cold-blooded animal with scaly skin

rival   animal that competes with another of the same kind, especially males fighting over a female

spawn   lay groups of eggs in the water

sperm   sex cells made by male animals

threat display   show of strength to warn away **rivals** and enemies

visual display   display that can be easily seen

vocal display   display using sound

Further Reading

Fredericks, Anthony D. and Sneed B. Collard. *Amazing Animals: Nature's Most Incredible Creatures.* Chanhassen, Minn.: Creative Publishing International, 2000.

Kalman, Bobbie. *How Do Animals Adapt?* New York: Crabtree Publishing, 2000.

Kalman, Bobbie. *What Are Camouflage and Mimicry?* New York: Crabtree Publishing, 2001.

Index